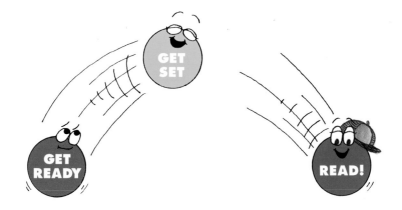

GET READY

GET SET

READ!

# JAKE AND THE SNAKE

*All inquiries should be addressed to:*
Barron's Educational Series, Inc.
250 Wireless Boulevard
Hauppauge, NY 11788

International Standard Book Number 0-8120-1732-3

Library of Congress Catalog Card Number 93-1015

**Library of Congress Cataloging-in-Publication Data**

Foster, Kelli C.
 Jake and the snake / by Foster & Erickson : illustrations by Keri
Gifford.
  p.  cm. — (Get ready—get set—read!)
 Summary: A snake helps Blake wake up Jake.
 ISBN 0-8120-1732-3
 (1. Sleep—Fiction. 2. Snakes—Fiction. 3. Stories in rhyme.)
I. Erickson, Gina Clegg, II. Gifford, Kerri, ill. III. Title.
IV. Series: Erickson, Gina Clegg. Get ready—get set—read!
PZ8.3.F813Jak   1993
(E)—dc20                                             93-1015
                                                       CIP
                                                       AC

PRINTED IN HONG KONG
19 18 17 16 15 14 13 12

GET READY…GET SET…READ!

# JAKE AND THE SNAKE

**by**
Foster & Erickson

**Illustrations by**
Kerri Gifford

**BARRON'S**

"Wake up Jake!"

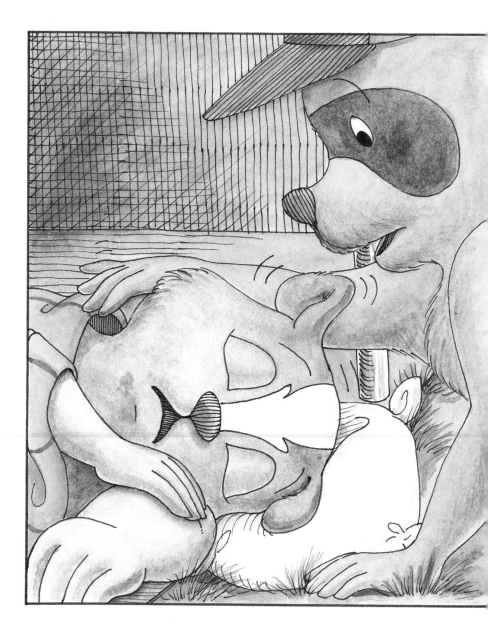

"I will give Jake
a little shake."

"I will make pancakes
to wake up Jake."

"Mmm…they are great!"

"Jake, you fake,
I know you are awake."

"I will take some water
from the lake."

"This should wake up Jake."

"What will it take to
wake up Jake?"

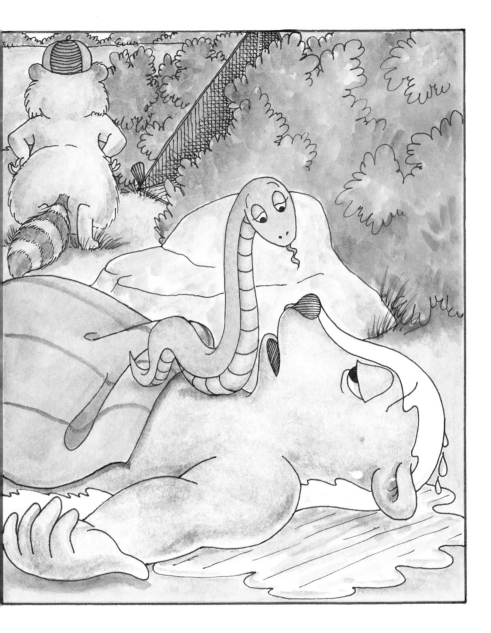

"A snake?"

"A snake!"

"Blake, Help!"
There is a snake."

"It was big and green
and will make you shake."

Blake finds the snake.

"Thank you, snake.
Now Jake is awake."

**The End**

# The AKE Word Family

awake
Blake
fake
Jake
lake
make
pancakes
shake
snake
take
wake

# Sight Words

now
you
give
know
some
they
finds
great
thank
there
water
should

## Dear Parents and Educators:

Welcome to *Get Ready...Get Set...Read!*

We've created these books to introduce children to the magic of reading.

Each story in the series is built around one or two word families. For example, *A Mop for Pop* uses the OP word family. Letters and letter blends are added to OP to form words such as TOP, LOP, and STOP. As you can see, once children are able to read OP, it is a simple task for them to read the entire word family. In addition to word families, we have used a limited number of "sight words." These are words found to occur with high frequency in the books your child will soon be reading. Being able to identify sight words greatly increases reading skill.

You might find the steps outlined on the facing page useful in guiding your work with your beginning reader.

We had great fun creating these books, and great pleasure sharing them with our children. We hope *Get Ready...Get Set...Read!* helps make this first step in reading fun for you and your new reader.

Kelli C. Foster, PhD
Educational Psychologist

Gina Clegg Erickson, MA
Reading Specialist

## Guidelines for Using *Get Ready...Get Set...Read!*

Step 1.     Read the story to your child.

Step 2.     Have your child read the Word Family list aloud
            several times.

Step 3.     Invent new words for the list. Print each new
            combination for your child to read. Remember,
            nonsense words can be used (*dat, kat, gat*).

Step 4.     Read the story *with* your child. He or she reads
            all of the Word Family words; you read the rest.

Step 5.     Have your child read the Sight Word list aloud
            several times.

Step 6.     Read the story *with* your child again. This time
            he or she reads the words from both lists; you
            read the rest.

Step 7.     Your child reads the entire book to you!

There are five sets of books in the

Series. Each set consists of five **FIRST BOOKS**
and two **BRING-IT-ALL-TOGETHER BOOKS**.

## SET 1

is the first set your children should read.
The word families are selected from the short vowel sounds:
**at**, **ed**, **ish** and **im**, **op**, **ug**.

## SET 2

provides more practice
with short vowel sounds:
**an** and **and**, **et**, **ip**, **og**, **ub**.

## SET 3

focuses on
long vowel sounds:
**ake**, **eep**, **ide** and **ine**, **oke** and **ose**, **ue** and **ute**.

## SET 4

introduces the idea that the word family sounds
can be spelled two different ways:
**ale/ail**, **een/ean**, **ight/ite**, **ote/oat**, **oon/une**.

## SET 5

acquaints children with word families that
do not follow the rules for long and short vowel sounds:
**all**, **ound**, **y**, **ow**, **ew**.